Helen Orme taught for many years before giving up teaching to write full-time. At the last count she had written over 70 books.

She writes both fiction and non-fiction, but at present is concentrating on fiction for older readers.

Helen also runs writing workshops for children and courses for teachers in both primary and secondary schools.

How many have you read?

Two years on:

Don't
Do It!

 Helen Orme

Ransom

Don' t Do It!
by Helen Orme
Illustrated by Chris Askham

Published by Ransom Publishing Ltd.
Radley House, 8 St. Cross Road, Winchester, Hampshire
SO23 9HX, UK
www.ransom.co.uk

ISBN   978 184167 744 6

First published in 2011

Meet the Sisters ...

Siti and her friends are really close. So close she calls them her Sisters. They've been mates for ever, and most of the time they are closer than her real family.

Siti is the leader – the one who always knows what to do – but Kelly, Lu, Donna and Rachel have their own lives to lead as well.

Still, there's no one you can talk to, no one you can rely on, like your best mates. Right?

1

A decent girlfriend

Siti and her friends were in the shopping centre.

Kelly wanted to buy clothes. She was going out with Gary that evening.

'How did you get Gary to take you out?' asked Donna.

Kelly had fancied Gary for ages. He liked her too, but he just wouldn't ask her out.

Kelly giggled. 'It's really funny,' she said. 'There's a girl in the year below me who fancies him. She won't leave him alone.'

'What's that got to do with him asking you out?' said Siti.

'Well, he got so fed up with it he asked Dan and Simon what to do.'

'I can't see either of them saying anything sensible,' said Lu.

'Simon told him the best way to get rid of her was to get a decent girlfriend, so that's why he asked me out.'

'That's mean,' said Siti. 'He's only asked you out to get rid of someone else.'

'No, not really,' said Kelly. 'You know what he's like. He just can't take the teasing from his mates, so when Simon suggested it – well they can't tease him now, can they?'

'I think that's sweet!' said Rachel.

2

Andy

At last Kelly got everything she wanted.

'I fancy a pizza,' said Siti.

The pizza place was full. They were lucky to find a table. They had just started eating when someone pushed by.

'Ouch!' said Siti, as someone bumped her arm. It was a nice-looking guy.

'Oh, sorry,' he said. He smiled at her.

'He's nice,' thought Siti. Then she noticed he was with a girl from their tutor group.

'Hiya Michelle,' she said.

'Oh, Hi. This is my cousin Andy and his mate Tom.'

She turned to Andy. 'These are some friends of mine – Siti and her Sisters!'

Michelle knew that Siti and her friends always called themselves 'The Sisters'.

Andy looked at Siti, then at the others. 'Er ...'

Siti laughed. 'She's teasing you,' she said. 'That's just a nickname.'

As they left, Donna whispered to Rachel. 'I think Siti fancies Andy. We'll have to try and get Michelle to bring him to the school disco.'

'He didn't look the type for school discos,' said Rachel. 'We'll have to think of some other idea to help Siti.'

But things didn't go quite as they planned.

3

'I've got to do something'

Christine Marker was Michelle's best friend. Kelly thought she might help them get to know Andy and Tom. She spoke to Chris in school.

'Have you met Michelle's cousin Andy?' she asked.

'Yeah,' Chris nodded. She didn't seem very keen.

'What's up?' asked Kelly.

'Oh, nothing,' said Chris. 'It's just that Michelle's spending all her time with Andy these days.'

'Don't you like him?'

'He's changed,' said Chris. 'So's Michelle.'

'What do you mean?' asked Kelly.

'She's just different. Sometimes everything's fine, but she gets into awful moods. Then she goes off by herself, or phones Andy. She doesn't want to hang around with me any more.'

Kelly talked to the Sisters.

'Not much hope for Siti then,' said Donna.

Siti laughed. 'I didn't fancy him anyway,' she said.

'Much!' said Donna. 'We saw how you looked at him.'

'Anyway, what can we do for Chris?' said Kelly. 'She's really upset about Michelle.'

'Well, she can hang around with us,' said Siti. 'Just till Michelle gets over whatever it is.'

The Sisters included Chris when they could. But she still wasn't happy.

'I'm really worried about Michelle,' she told them. 'She's bunking off school now.'

'She wasn't in science yesterday,' said Lu. 'I thought she wasn't very well.'

'She doesn't look well,' said Rachel.

'I'm going to talk to her,' said Chris. 'I've got to do something!'

4

Getting really bad

'She won't even talk to me now,' Chris told the Sisters. She was crying. 'I said I wanted to help, but she just bit my head off.'

'She's changed so much,' said Lu. 'She used to be good fun. Now she's just a misery.'

'Have you been round to her house?' asked Siti.

'I did,' said Chris. 'But she pushed me out and swore at me. She'd got Andy and Tony there and she definitely didn't want me around.'

'What is the matter with her?' asked Siti. 'Is everything O.K. at home?'

'I suppose so,' said Chris. 'No, I'm sure it's not home. It's something to do with those boys.'

'We've got to find out what,' said Siti. 'We can't help unless we know.'

They all watched Michelle. Sometimes she was happy and would talk. Other times she blanked everyone.

She wasn't doing well in class either and the teachers kept on at her.

One day things got really bad.

Mrs Williams was having a go at her for not doing her English homework.

'This just isn't good enough ... !' But before she could go on, Michelle stood up.

'I don't care,' she yelled. 'You're just a stupid old woman in a stupid school. You can all go and ...'

She burst into tears and rushed out.

'Well,' said Mrs Williams. 'I'll deal with her later. Now, we'd better get on.'

5

Is anyone in there?

Luckily it was almost break time.

'Where should we look?' asked Siti. 'Rachel and Donna, go and check the form room. Lu and Kelly have a look outside.'

She turned to Chris. 'We'll check the loos.'

They couldn't find Michelle anywhere. Then Chris had an idea.

'What about that disabled toilet round the back of the hall?' she said.

When they got there, the door was locked.

Siti knocked. 'Hello,' she called. 'Is anyone in there?'

There was no answer. Siti listened at the door.

'I can hear something,' she said.

Chris listened too.

'Someone's throwing up,' she said. 'I bet it's Michelle.'

Siti knocked again. 'Michelle, we know it's you. Open the door.'

No answer.

Then Chris tried. 'Come on Michelle,' she called. 'It's me and Siti.'

At first they thought she just wasn't going to answer. Siti had just decided to go and find her dad when the door opened.

Michelle looked at them.

'Help me,' she said. 'I feel awful. I think I'm going to die.'

6

Miss Giles understands

'Come with us,' said Siti. 'We'll find my dad. He'll help.'

Siti's dad was the deputy head. Michelle didn't want to see him!

'No!' Michelle tried to pull away.

'Who can we take her to?' Chris whispered to Siti.

Siti thought quickly. 'Let's go to Mrs Williams. She'll listen. And if we can get it sorted she might not do anything about Michelle being rude.'

Chris put her arm round Michelle, but Michelle collapsed onto the floor.

'You stay with her,' Siti told Chris. 'I'll go and get someone.'

She ran off. 'I'd better find Dad,' she thought. 'She looks really bad.'

But the first teacher she met was Miss Giles.

She looked at Siti. 'What's the matter?' she asked.

Siti was so worried she didn't care who she told.

'It's Michelle Robinson,' she said. 'She's ill, really ill.'

'Show me.'

Siti turned back. 'Of all the teachers,' she thought. 'Why did it have to be her?'

Miss Giles was nice, but usually she was totally useless.

When they got back Michelle was sitting up, but still looked bad. Chris looked even worse!

Miss Giles bent down to Michelle. 'What's the matter?' she asked gently.

It was Chris who answered. 'Drugs!' she said.

Miss Giles was brilliant. Siti was amazed.

'Go to the office and get them to call an ambulance,' she said. 'As she's been so sick she'll probably be O.K., but we can't take chances.'

Chris was glad to go.

'Well,' said Miss Giles, looking at Michelle. 'Do you want to tell me about it?'

Michelle burst into tears. 'It was Tom. He kept giving me stuff. He said it wouldn't hurt me. It was just for fun.'

'But it does hurt, doesn't it?' said Miss Giles. 'How long have you been doing it?'

'Not long,' said Michelle. 'I'm not sure. But I'm an addict now, aren't I? What am I going to do?'

Miss Giles looked at Siti. 'Do you know how long?'

Siti shrugged. 'I don't think it's many weeks,' she said.

'Listen to me,' said Miss Giles. 'If it's only a short time you can be helped easily. You've just got to be strong.'

'I can't,' sobbed Michelle.

'You can,' said Miss Giles. 'And I'll help.'

'How can you help? You don't know what it's like!'

'Yes I do,' said Miss Giles. She looked at Siti. 'You mustn't tell anyone this,' she said.

'But I do understand. When I was a student I got hooked. I thought I'd never get off drugs. I thought I'd ruined my life.'

'That's what I've done,' said Michelle.

'But you haven't, any more than I have,' said Miss Giles firmly. 'Look at me now. You'd never guess would you?'

There was no time to say any more. Chris was back.

'Is she O.K. to go to the office?' she asked. 'I've got to tell them if she's not.'

Michelle got up. 'I think so,' she said. She looked at Miss Giles. 'Thank you.'

'Come and see me, soon,' said Miss Giles. 'Now let's get you seen to.'

Later Siti and Chris told the Sisters the details. But there was one important fact that Siti kept a secret.

'It was a pity it was Miss Giles you found,' said Rachel. 'She's so drippy.'

'You know,' said Siti 'I think she was the best of all.'

And that was all she would say.